JN441299

Green Magic

What If You Can Reduce Carbon Emissions?

Dedicated to

Il-Je, Jo, ex-professor of Pusan National University who has given me a lot of advice on English Education and daily life.
Eung-Mo, Yeo, principal of Jangan High School who has helped me keep on studying.
Ae-Ryun Yi, Jeong-Min Seo, and Yeong-Bok Jeong et el., my students, who helped choose the proper words.
Byeong-Do, Kim, ex SME advisory consultant.
Chae-Oh, Im, who was the chairman of North District Council of Ulsan Metropolitan City.
Dong-Hun, Jang, who was a GTEP professor of Dankuk University.
Deok-Su Kim, head teacher of Jinju Bongwon Middle School who has given me some advice on the grammar and the storylines.
Eun-Seon Kim, ex-teacher of National/Public Manchon Boseong Childcare Center.
Hye-Jin Kang, English instructor of Jaesong Elementary and Mujeong Elementary.
In-Yul, Choi, who works as a director as well as a doctor in Hyemin clinic.
Ji-Eon, Ga-Eon, and Seung-Eon Yeo, my daughters, who helped arrange storylines.
Jin-Hwan Park, retirement design expert who works for Samsung Life Insurance Co., Ltd.
Gab-Seon, Son and Ssang-Soon, Park, who have helped me keep on studying.
Gi-Yeong, Park, who works as a supervisor in Sacheon Office of Education.
Gyeongsang Time Association alumni and students—especially PG5—for the energy they give me.
Gyung, Kang, who works as the deputy director of nutrition department in Busan Adventist Hospital.
Keun-Saeng Park, principal of Jinyang High School who worked as the head of Hapcheon Office of Education.
Seong-Hyub, Han, professor of Pusan Women's University who has rooted for making up the story for young adults.
Sook-Kyung Son, Medical Administrative Staff who takes care of my physical health.
Soon-Yeo Yi, English instructor who has given me some advice on the grammar.
Woon-Kyung, Kim, who worked as an English teacher at Changwon Machinery and Technology High School.
Woong-Gon, Seong, vice principal of Samlangjin Elementary School who has given me a lot of support.
Yeon-Ok Park, counseling psychologist who takes care of my mental health.
Young-Ok Jo, vice director as well as English instructor who helped me choose proper words.

Pictures by Eun-woo Shin

Green Magic

What If You Can Reduce Carbon Emissions?

by **Mi-heui Jeong**
Pictures by **En-woo Shin**

PNUPRESS

Does the Earth forget spring?

April sunlight, cold as ice, quietly seeps into the room of the twins, Carbon and Carbae.

Carbon is making a call to Moss.

"Hello, Moss. This is Carbon.
Where are you?"

“I’m coming
with Cheolsu.”

“We’re going there by bike.
We’re 12 km away from
Bujeon station.”

"Okay, Moss.
Let's meet by the bike rack
in front of Bujeon station."

"Riding a bike makes us feel great
and can even help us avoid traffic jams.
See you later!"

"Wake up, Carbae.
Today is the field trip day!
Moss and Cheolsu are
coming now."

"What time is it now? Today is the day to do a science project titled What If We Can Reduce Carbon Emissions?."

“Right. It’s ten thirty.
We are supposed to meet
Cheolsu and Moss at eleven o’clock.”

"Sorry, I overslept!
Let's make some soybean stew
and salad right away. Just wait a bit."

"Brunch is ready.
Help yourself,
Carbon."

"Thanks, Carbea.
So delicious."

"Now I'm going to fill the tumbler with water."

"I will delete unwanted messages and images."

"Now let's separate our trash and put it in the recycling bin."

“That sounds good.
I will leave some of the trash
behind for upcycling.”

“Almost ready to go out, Carbea?”

"Sure. Let's put a thin jacket in our backpacks. The weather forecast says it will be a little cold this morning."

상장

"I will turn off the lights,
Carbea."

"Okay. I will unplug cords which are not in use."

Moss is making a call to Carbon.

부 전 역
“Yes, we are coming.
Look up at the stairs.”

"Sounds good."

"Let's take the train
that leaves at 11:20."

“Okay. Let’s check our preparations. We brought two little pine trees and trowels.”

"We brought writing materials."

"And some water."

"Let's go to Gijang to plant pine trees."

“Younghee will pick us up at Gijang station.”

"Let's set, go!"

"Go!"

Thirty minutes later,
Moss shouts passing by Songjeong.

"Look out the window. There's an eco-friendly building that uses solar power."

Younghee is waiting Cheolsu and his friends at the parking lot near Gijang station.

Then she gives them a ride to get to Yonggungsa at an economic speed rate of 50 km per hour.

"Okay."
"Thanks for the ride, Younghee."
"Guys, here we are. Could you please get out of the car?"

"You're welcome."

"The sea whispers and
the sky bows in silence."

"Wow, this is Younggungsa.
How beautiful it is!"

"Ha, ha!"
"Cheolsu is talking like a poet."

"Let's plant pine trees on our way to Sirangdae
after a 15-minute tour around here."

侍郞臺

"Look over here. That pine tree is dead.
Let's plant these pine trees around here."

"We dig a hole, put a pine tree in each hole, fill it with dirt, and tamp down the dirt."
"We're finished."

"Make sure Sirangdae and the pine trees are in view, Cheolsu."

"Oh, the wind is blowing hard all of a sudden."

"Just moment.
I'll try again.
By the way,
Moss is missing."

"Moss, Moss, where are you?
I can't find you anywhere."

"Carbon! Carbae! I am here on your skin.
I was reborn and am growing there."

"Oh, I can't believe it.
Did you disappear with
wrapping paper that
covered the pine trees?"

"Are you okay, Moss?"

"Yes. Both the paper and I instantly went with the wind. Then I was reborn as moss."

"Do you think Moss can come with us to Ulsan for the field trip tomorrow? I'm a bit worried."
"Yeah, I'm worried, too."

“We’re supposed to do
a carbon-capture and
storage project there.”

"Don't worry about it. I am always with you. A small effort of each will lead to a great achievement."

"I am glad to hear that from you,
Moss. We all had a great time."

"Our first green field trip is done.
Cheolsu, look around.
You are green, too."

"Really? Young-hee,
you are much greener.
If we all reduce carbon
emissions, the world
will be..."

"That's it.
We will be green
and so will the
environment."

"Then we can green
anyone, and be
greened endlessly."

"Then the earth
will never forget
spring. See you
tomorrow."
"Surely. If every day is
green, tomorrow will
be green, too."

They lived an eco-friendly life for a year like that, so finally warm spring returned.

"I love the spring sunshine."

Green Magic

What If You Can Reduce Carbon Emissions?

1st Edition Issued, January 23, 2026.
1st Edition Printed, February 13, 2026.

Printed in the Rep. of KOREA
Author Miheui Jeong
Illustrator Eun-woo Shin
Designer Youngmi Bae
Publisher Jaewon Choi
Published by Pusan National University Press

Publication Registration No. 1983-000001 November 10, 1983
2, Busandaehak-ro 63beon-gil, Geumjeong-gu, Busan, 46241, Rep. of KOREA
Tel +82 051 510 1932
Fax +82 051 512 7812
https://press.pusan.ac.kr

ISBN 978-89-7316-857-6 (07810)